John

MW01138944

The Irishman Part 2

Introduction to the Author

John Francis "The Irishman" is written by Sean Collins aka John Francis Sullivan Jr, the novel is based on true story's and real events. There is information in this book that is fictitious, and names have been changed for the need of anonymity of others.

This novel is Part Two of a series that will provide information on growing up on Smith Hill and Federal Hill in Providence RI. It will also provide inside information on crime and corruption based on personal experiences of John Francis Sullivan Jr aka Sean Collins. These experiences also include personal conversations he had with many people who were allegedly involved in organized crime and police he had grown up with on Smith Hill. He had personal relationships with many of these people because of his minimal involvement in organized crime and his Dad's association in organized crime on a national level in the NY Mafia.

Part One was about the JFK and Hoffa Conspiracy's and my Dad and Uncle Frank's involvement.

Dedication

John Francis The Irishman Part Two is dedicated to the Families of Smith Hill where I grew up. The Simoneau, Young, Tarasanko, Burns, Hart, Cromwell, Guertin, Corio, Hickey, Ryan, Santos, Rainey, Bennett, Holt, Pontarelli, Brearley, Cheski, McCauley, O Connor, Grenier, Sparks , Ornazian ,Feeney ,Root, Tracy, Brady, Hassett, Cambell, Ahern, Russo , Noonans, McGurn,

Kaplin, Bohan, Sandburg ,MacCloud, Bussman, Angel ,Howe, Rodgers, Corry, Fortune , Walsh, Cains, Holt, Williams, Petrone, Dutra, Roberts, Grant, Capuano, Gayners, Manfredi, Leddy, Hopper, Gavuillen, Ray, Randells, Richardsons, O'Neill, Esposito, Sullivan, Grant, Collins, Perez, Quinn, Ramos, Lanigan, Barnes, Dolen, Harrington, Cychevic, Ward, Campbell, Whelan, Morrissey, Murray, Davis, McCormick, Smith, Brophy, Boyle, Goodwin, Hagen, Quick, Richardson, Bucci, Sousa, Tessitore, Bagian, Tetreault, DeRenius, Chobanian, Keegan, Farange, Batey, Cockley, Almedia, Morgan, Perry, Thomas, Keegan, Tillinghast, Swider, Cokley, and many more that I may have forgot my memory hits a blank sometimes.

Also, the many friends and families that have made a different in my life that lived on Federal Hill where I spent 20 years living on and off before leaving for Florida. Many families took me in like I was part of their family, Bucci, Melise, Passarelli, DelSanto, Patriarca, Bianco, DelGesso, Lasorsa, Marrapese, and all the many neighbors on Ridge St, Penn St, Federal St, Gesler St and Atwells Ave.

Living on Federal Hill was interesting to say the least, from being awoke several times a night by the passing trains on Ridge St in Ronnie Passarelli's house. Penn and Knight St brought the wise guys playing crap in the alley and the hilarious running and jumping over fences they did when the cops would try to raid the game. They were dressed in expensive suits and shiny shoes and would slide and fall and curse trying to get away. Soon I was working as a lookout on Knight St, and my job was to watch for the cops and signal that they were on their way. The cops arrested me a few times for doing that, being a juvenile, they had to let me go with a beating most of the time. The guys would throw me a ten spot for the night or more if the cops grabbed me.

Living on Federal Hill was like the 'Good Fella' movie, it was the Mecca of organized crime in New England. Raymond's office on Atwells Ave was like city hall everything went through the 'Office' were Raymond would stand outside or in the front window watching the world go by. Until being heard on the first wiretap by Kennedy's in the 60s Raymond would have many people coming and going all day long. After the wiretap he would walk outside to the alley and stroll as he was doing business. Years later working for the City of Providence Anthony Melise and I would visit the office and see if Raymond had any requests from residents on the hill for us to do like trash or potholes. He was like the Mayor they would call him first before calling the city because he would always solve their problems.

People hear the words organized crime or gangster and mobsters hold those involved with distain. It was my experience that most were stand up guys and always very respectful to me. Raymond was like a grandfather to me and the rest of the guys were like Uncles to me. Always telling me to stay out of trouble and don't be like them because I was a smart kid.

All the bad stuff you would read about in Providence Journal front page weekly newspaper was mostly about business in organized crime. Everyone involved knew the rules and the ones that broke the rules because of greed or becoming 'Rats' paid with their life.

The police in RI and the Feds were incredible 'Corrupt' they did and said anything that would suit there needs to build a case against anyone involved in anything organized crime or not. Rhode Island has had more politicians, judges, and law enforcement officials charged with corruption and jailed in many cases than any other state in history. RI is the smallest state in the union.

Growing up on Smith Hill

      Growing up in Providence Rhode Island was interesting to say the least. I lived on Smith Hill my first 17 years near the state capital which was the Irish side of town. Growing up on Smith Hill was both a burden and an amazing learning experience. Growing up on the tough streets of Smith Hill made you grow up early in your life. Having seen two young friends drown at the age of eight was an eye-opening experience and opened the door for what was my first PTSD experience. Already a child who was hyperactive and could not sit still this event had me all over the place and always in trouble. I look back and say I was the worse child ever, punished every day of my childhood till the age of 12 or so. I was not allowed to play with other kids in school or after school in the play grounds. I was an angry child that was mad at my parents for divorcing when I was five years old. At age five I went to live with my Nana for next 12 years and never lived with my parents again. For the most part I got rid of the anger when I discover sports and basketball to burn off all my energy.

My Grandmother was the rock that held our very large extended family together. Nana had outlived two husbands over the years and was a widow when I arrived on her doorstep. There were the Hagen's from her first marriage the Sullivan's from the second marriage for a total of eight children. Those produced 27 grandchildren and over 54 great grandchildren. My Nana's home was like the center of universe for the family and the neighborhood. We all lived within four or five blocks of each other. There were the Collins, Sullivan's, Corry's, Bannon's, McGinns and the Randell's family's that were part of our Irish Clan.

Smith Hill was an integrated neighborhood of many black and white families. There were many Irish, Polish, Jewish, Armenian family's along with hundreds of black families. I have made numerous lifelong friendships with Smith Hillers that still remain today with help from Face Book and other social media outlets.

There are too many names to list them all here and not forget someone who was a part of my life at some time growing up on Smith Hill. Smith Hill is where the state house and capital of Rhode Island stands. The State House was 200 yards from my childhood home on Holden St. We would play baseball, football, and any other number of crazy games there on the grounds in summer and use our sleds in cold of winter to go down the steep hills.

The State house itself was our playground at times until security would chase us away. We would climb the winding staircase up 300 feet to the top of the dome and go outside and view all of Providence on a clear day. We would sneak into the tombs in the basement of the capital and follow them down to the waterfront openings were the ships used to unload cargo a hundred years earlier. Most of us were scared shitless to going in these dark rooms and caverns unground but we went anyways nobody wanted to be called "Chicken". My cousin Kevin Randell was usually the leader of the pack, he was fearless he always did everything first, jump off this building, climb the railroad tower, go into the big sewer pipes on Pleasant Valley Parkway that were underground threw whole city of Providence.

Many of us came from single parent homes or being raised by grandmothers as I was. No one had much money, and all came from working class families. So, we found a million ways to get in trouble and some cases put our self's in grave danger, as Kevin and I did one day down near the Fox Point Bridge and the Providence River met. We had gone down there because a small whale which they named "Willy" the Whale had come into the river and had died in the shallow water sometime earlier that month. Well tragedy struck this day when the Plante brothers fell into the river and got stuck in the muck which was the Providence River at the time. Kevin and I tried to save them to avail. I ran up the road and jumped in front of an auto to get them to stop and help us. Kevin stayed at the wall swinging his belt trying to pull them out. By the time the adult and I reached the water the oldest brother was going down below the surface. Both brothers drowned right there in front of Kevin and me. We grew up fast on Smith Hill.

Davis Park, Retard Park, Danforth Rec Center, Smith Hill Drop Inn, Smith St School and St Patrick's School basketball courts is where we lived for most of our early childhoods when not stuck in the house being punished for some bonehead incident which in my case was many.   A lot of my problem was that when someone dared me on something crazy I could not let that slide and do something crazy that would find me in trouble and my Dad having to pay to fix something I had broken on a dare.

On one Halloween night my cousin Billy Corry dared me to throw a pumpkin through Goldburgs Pharmacy door window, so I picked the largest pumpkin of the batch and let it fly and ran my tail off home. Dad had to pay $ 28 which in the 1960s was a lot of money. I did not see the life of day for quite a while after that one

I attended three schools in my first five years of schooling. St Ann's' was the first were I stayed back in the first grade, on to St Casmirs and finally St Patrick's. Trouble would follow me were ever I went; anger and hyperactivity would be my daily battles.

I could write all day about all the crazy things we did growing up on Smith Hill but will just talk about my first good friends and how we run from one area of the city to the other looking for things to do. Sports was always the center of our day, whether it was basketball, baseball, or football. My first crew of friends included my cousins Billy Corry, Eddy Bannon, Donald Feeney,

Alan Tarasanko, Jonny Russo, and Mark Cromwell. We would play on Bernon St, Violet St, and down at Davis Park.Billy and Donald were like the leaders of the pack and were the oldest of our crew.

In the 60s and 70s basketball was king in Providence with the great Providence College Teams that were one of top ranked teams in the country for over a decade. Plus, this was when the Boston Celtics were the world champs 15 years. Our middle school St Patrick's was the best basketball program in the state and always chasing state championships every year on four grade levels. St Pats was coached by Joe Hassett a legend in New England basketball, Joe was like a second father to me and included me in a lot of his family activities.

Basketball kept a lot of kids in school because most of us came from very dysfunctional families were alcohol ruled the day in many families. Many single parent families or children being raised by grandmothers or other family members. Our pride in our basketball program at St Pats was the single most important thing in a lot of our lives. We had this small little band box gym where we were almost unbeatable for a dozen years or so. I had been undefeated in the four years I played for St Pats. Many of us looked it as our way out of the neighborhood and a way to get a better education and be offered scholarships to private high schools and colleges. Many succeeded and several made it to the NBA and MLB.

I was on path to chase my dreams to college until 1968 when I was 15 and the Pizza World shooting occurred were my best friend Eddy Brady was shot and the shooter tried to kill me over an issue he had with my Dad. Eddy survived but it took several years for him to recover. As for me the nightmare of reliving the shooting every night caused me to start drinking just to fall asleep sent me off the deep end. This was the second PTSD event of my first 15 years and I never recovered from it for many years.

      With basketball in the rear-view mirror because you had to attend school to play softball became my outlet now to use my skills as a good athlete and one that could run like a deer. Playing softball was also a way for me to drink beer at all of Smith Hills bars free. In my second year playing I played on a men's team that won a state championship under the name of Harrys Tap. Everyone one was much older than me and being one of the top players I always drank for free. I know today I was an alcoholic from the first time I drank when after drinking two quarts of Narragansett Beer I threw up and almost died in my sleep yet wanted to drink again. I was not an everyday drinker but whenever I drank I could not stop until money ran out, bar closed, or passed out into a blacked out.

      Smith Hill tap was my favorite bar on Smith Hill. The tap was owed by Walter Ladish and his son John Ladish who has been a lifelong friend of mine. John is an amazing chef and cooked for my second wedding to Maryellen which must have been lucky because we are still together today 32 years later.

      I started working for Walter when I was 17 as a bartender even though drinking age was 21 at the time. I went into the Army for 18 months and came home at 20 and worked at the tap as my second job. To Walters surprise John and the guys threw a birthday party for me when I turned 21 and was finally legal to drink in RI. Walter almost shit his pants that I was underage all those years. Soon afterwards the state changed the drinking age to 18 and we all had a good laugh at that.

The Tap was the center of the universe for my group of 30 or so of my friends. Many of us were vets of the Viet Nam War and drank to forget what we had saw as very young men. There were many cops, firemen, city workers and state workers in our group of misfits. There were many a fight among ourselves in the Tap that we would laugh about the next day. There were yearly trips to Fenway to see the Sox play and that was a drinking holiday for all. Walter Ladish had his hands full especially after the game we would stop at a fancy restaurant for steak dinners which turned into a brawl with other bus full of drunks. John Ladish had to stay half way sober to baby sit many of us wackos. Lots of very good memories from the Smith Hill Tap days and many of our close friends died way too early in their journey of life. Donald Feeney, Donald McGurn, Billy and Bobby Corry to name a few that was very hard to deal with and broke our hearts. I can still smell the hot dogs that Walter and John would cook every weekend that fed everyone, so we did not spend money on food more to drink. There were many professional drinkers at the Tap and I was not one of them, I had to take speeders to keep up with the pros, so I could make it through the weekend and not get sick. The women we were married to back then were saints to put up with us. We all worked two jobs all week and drank all weekends. Many divorces in the 70s for many of us.

There were bars on every block it seemed on Smith Hill, sometimes several. The first famous one was The Dew Drop Inn which was taken down for interstate 95 in the 60s. American Legion, Busy Bee, Curran and McCailes, Dug Out, Polish Club, Armenian Club, Lithuanian Club, Peter and Pauls, Harrys Tap, Alibi, and last but not least Smith Hill Tap. There were several others that slipped my mind because I did not visit them all.

I tell the tale that they put beer in our baby bottles when we were young instead of milk, because alcoholics ruled every family. Which caused a lot of grief for many families over the years. In spite the many issues and hardships many went through it was a great place to grow up in and learn the ropes of life which it prepared us well for.

It taught us that in life in RI it was important who you were, who you knew, were you were from. If you were willing to work hard and never take no for an answer you can make it in life. Many Smith Hillers have made great successes of their lives and I am very proud of all considering were we all started out. Many had the odds against them in the beginning put kept moving forward.

Many of my childhood friends and family have died too early in their lives. This has made me to travel to Providence and shed many a tear to many times over the years. Billy Corry and Donald Feeney two of my childhood friends just broke my heart when I returned to help bury them. One was like my older brother in Billy and Donald was like my mentor who helped guide me through some crazy events in my life. I loved them both dearly. I lost 2 Italians from Federal Hill that were rocks in my life, my Brother in Law Tony Bucci, who saved my life along with my sister Marge when my Grandmother passed away. They provided a roof over my head when I had been living on the street getting in all sorts of problems. Marge help me get my city jobs and always watched over me. Tony was also my best man at my second marriage to Maryellen who he was very fond of and bring a smile to his face each time he saw her.

Anthony Melise was my boss, best friend, cousin, and kindest guy walking the earth. And did he always have my back. It broke my heart when they both passed away neck surgery and could not fly. I grieved alone at home in Florida reliving all the great memory's we shared.

Trouble in Providence Politics

Early in 1973, a few weeks before Joe Doorley presided over the Civic Center grand opening ,which was Doorley dream come true which he fought for to have built for over a decade. The Civic Center was to be the centerpiece of rebuilding downtown Providence. Providence College basketball was at it peak at that time. Two local kids Ernie D.and Marvin Barnes had put Providence back on top by reaching the NCAA semi finals.But as anything goes in Providence there is always stories corruption and kick-backs everywere. And this was no different and became Buddy Cianci's opportunity to get his foot in the door of Providence politics.

Harald Copeland Doorley's choice to be the first director of the Civic Center, was caught on tape asking for a $1000 brib from Skip Chernov the promoter of the Grateful Dead concert. Chernov takes the tape to Rhode Island attorney general Richard Israel, who assigned the case to junior prosecuter Buddy Cianci.

This event is what opened the door for Buddy Cianc's political career in Providence.. Cianci sensed the winds of discontent going through the mighty Democratic Party. Rhode Island state police set up a sting to get Copeland except the money but he did not go for it. Copeland had been warned by Doorley it was a setup.This was right about the time that the Watergate scandal was mushrooming in the country,and Doorley knew that the Republicans attempt to bug the Democratic National Committee offices was no shock to him so he was very leary.

Cianci took advantage of the internal war that was going on between Doorley and Mr Democrat, Larry McGarry who was the long time king maker in Providence politics. McGarry felt that Doorley had lost touch with the man on the street that had put him in office for ten years. Some said Doorley had reneged on a promise to run for higher office and open the door up for another McGarry protégé. In summer of 1973 McGarry's Democratic City Committee refused to endorse Doorley for reelection in 1974.

In the fall of 1973 prosecutor Buddy Cianci presented the case of Harald Copeland to a state grand jury. On October 10, Copeland was indicted for soliciting a bribe. Doorley claimed it was 'politically motivated' and turned out to be the begging of the end for Doorley.

By then ,Cianci was actively running for mayor of Providence.Cianci soon resigned from the AG office. He called himself the anticorruption canidate.Through the summer and fall all eyes were on the Democratic fight between Doorley and McGarry's chosen canidate Francis Brown. Doorley won the primary by 2000 votes

A group of Brown supporters pulled together to join up with Buddy Cianci for the general election and called themselves Democrats for Cianci which I was a part of. Cianci went on to win the general election by 200 or so votes.He became the first Italian American Mayor of Providence...And the rest is history when it comes to the legacy of Buddy Cianci.

Mad Dog & Genovese Family

Threw out the 1970s Dad spent a lot of time in
NYC working with Russell Bufalina and the Genovese
family one of the five familys that controled everything
in Western NYC. Dad was trying to sit on a fence
because he was friendly with the upstart Irish Westies
who were becoming a power of there own in labor and
loan sharking and other violent crimes. They were a
wild and crazy bunch of guys and making trouble for the
Genovese family of which Dad was a important
associate in setting up hits in the city. Dad would get
orders from Russell Bufilino the acting head of the

family.Dad would then give the contract to operaters like "Joseph Mad Dog Sullivan" who was no relation to our family.Mad Dog was one of the worse killers in American history, having killed up to a hundred mobsters on contracts for Genovese family. Sullivan was thought to haved killed eight members of the Westies including Mickey Spillane the leader, Tom Devaney,and the Butcher Edward Commisky all in Hell Kitchen. His final hit was John Fiorino who was a made man and a teamsters official.   He asked for Dad's help but Dad had cut him loose because he was a loose cannon.Mad Dog was captured and giving life with no parole.

.

Jerry & George

My friend Jerry Tillinghast was accused in several underworld murders in RI and New York City. Jerry worked for the Patriarca crime family in Providence RI.

Unfortunately, on November 30, 1977 his underworld career came to a screeching halt when Jerry and his older brother Harold were arrested for killing a mob loan shark, George Basmajian, aka George Lombardi. George was a childhood friend who went to St Pat's Grammar school the 1960s and was

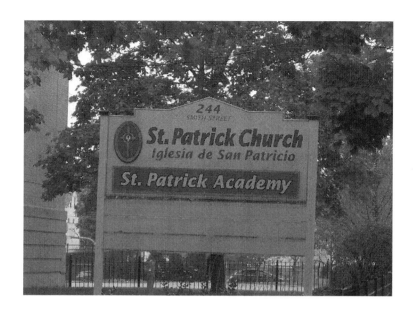

in my homeroom. George hung around with all the Irish and Italian kids and was treated badly until he began lifting weights and got into kickboxing. He eventually became the New England Heavyweight Kick -Box Champion.

Well George started hanging around with Matty G, an up and coming wise guy in the Mob. So Matty put George in his little crew, but it did not take George long to grow tired of being used to putting the fear of God into people and learning the ways of "La Cosa Nostra". George thought he was bigger and tougher than everyone else and wanted to do things his way. George finally got hooked up with Gerard "The Frenchman" Ouimette, who was helping run the Mob from prison at the ACI. George visited the Frenchmen in jail, and getting to know him, he started doing some small assignments cracking a couple of heads of guys that were not paying up.

George was never satisfied. He was always looking for recognition. George started going back and forth to NYC running assignments for the Frenchman who had just got out of jail. George was dealing with John Gotti and his Ozone Park crew.

George started thinking that he was somebody who had to start pushing his weight around. George had a partner named Caesar who was another karate guy, and they got into a beef with a couple of guys and they killed them both. George and Caesar started having their own issues. Turned out Caesar was dating a Capo's niece and George would have to get permission to do anything to Caesar to avoid getting himself in trouble. Well before Raymond Sr, gave any permission for anything, Caesar disappeared. Everyone thought he was out of town. Then his car was found in Warwick hotel parking lot. In the trunk was Caesar body, shot a few times in the head.

A few days later George was called in to the office to talk to Raymond Sr. He had a smile on his face and said he'd done everyone a favor. Raymond was appalled, and George's ass was grass, as they say.

George was killed in a stolen car at TF Green airport. The FBI and state police had been tailing the stolen car that night of the shooting but lost it for a few moments and that's when the killing occurred. They believed Jerry and his brother Harald were in the car with George. The FBI and State Police caught up with them an hour later and arrested them. After the trial, they were given life in prison. Jerry was released in 2008, and Harold died from cancer.

Jerry, George, Harold and I were all friends, and Jerry never wanted me to go down the road that George travelled. In doing so he paid the ultimate price with his life. That could have been me if I had not taken the advice Jerry had given to me earlier.

Harold claimed 'til the day he died he was innocent and was not with his brother that night but sitting in the bar that Jerry had returned to on Broadway, there were several witnesses that backed him up to no avail.

Bob Ricci Saga

As you can tell by my previous novel my Dad operated on the opposite side of the law, from traditional law enforcement agencies. But growing up in Providence Rhode Island he had many close friends from both sides of the law that he had great respect for, and vice versa. There was mutual respect, The Mob never fucked with the cops because it was bad for business. The Mob in return expected fairness, and in many cases paid for that fairness in the form of warnings when something was coming down on someone.

Bob Ricci was a good honest cop that my Dad knew and respected for many years, along with Jacky Leyden and Teddy Collins two cops he grew up with on

Smith Hill. My Dad was very upset with the way Bob Ricci was pressured into taking his own life.

In 1978, Buddy Cianci was re-elected Mayor for a second term. It proved to be much easier than his first election with thousands of absentee ballots and our photo ID program we had used in 1974, but at a much smaller level, because the polls had him way ahead.

Cianci was running around the country trying to make a big name for himself on a national level within the Republican Party. He had given a speech at the Republican Convention for Gerald Ford and was trying to be the first Italian-American nominated for a high-level position in the Republican Party. But back in Providence several of the mayor's men were also celebrating their constitutional rights, most notably the right to be presumed innocent and the right against self-incrimination.

Bob Ricci was made Chief of Police in Providence, which was the second largest police department in New England, when he thought being a police officer was about chasing criminals. Ricci was a beat cop who grew up on the south side of the city and rose through the ranks developing a reputation for incorruptibility as the head of the C-Squad, which fought drugs, prostitution and gambling, and was a pain in the ass to many of us in the numbers business.

Ricci now had other problems dealing with Buddy Cianci and his meddling in the hiring of police officer recruits into the new police academy. Cianci had pressed him to admit five recruits, whom the police selection board had rejected. As a result, three were admitted and the other two filed lawsuits against the city. One of those two was named Eddy C. He was an aide and driver for Buddy Cianci and a city employee. I knew Eddy personally and knew that he had some issues from his past because he was close to my Italian family up on Federal Hill, so we all understood the problem.

The issue had come up the previous year with the selection of Fire Recruits and the number of Blacks and Hispanic that were not chosen just because they were minorities, and Federal Law Suits were filed. Some white candidates were by passed because of their race.

A growing number of police officers said privately that Cianci had politicized the police department more than any mayor in the past. They pointed out the arrest of City Council President Bobby Haxton, an enemy of Cianci, on moral charges by police that some feel had set him up. Bob Ricci did not do well with all the political pressure put upon him. Politics had no place in Ricci's life, which revolved around his family and his job. He saw things in black and white, not grey. Ricci who knew every thief and bookie in Providence did not know how to deal with Cianci.

Ricci was worried about having to testify in court about the police school selections. He did not want to lie on the stand. this was told to me by Teddy Collins, a family friend who was a police officer and close assistant to Commander Ricci.

On a stormy Friday evening Ricci had told Teddy Collins and other officers that he was going to quit and could not take it anymore. He had thought the job was

29

chasing bad guys, he could not figure out the politics of it all.

Late on Monday night, January 16, 1978, Ricci told his wife he had to go to the office. A short time later, he called her back and asked her to call Collins and Jackie Leyden, another friend of my fathers, and ask them to come to the station and to Ricci's office, he needed them. When they arrived, they found Ricci dead in his inner office with a gunshot wound to his head. He had left a note saying it all was too much, and asks Jackie Leyden to take care of his family.

Later when Cianci was notified, he was said to be shaken up by Ronnie Glantz, but also asked if Ricci had left a note and if it mentioned him. Cianci showed up at the police station a few hours later where tough guy cops fought back tears, and many said that Cianci deserved much of the blame. Cianci called this the saddest day he had experienced as mayor. He declared a 30 day of mourning and ordered flags lowered to half-staff.

Well a few days after Ricci was buried, the shit hit the fan when my father's friend, Captain Teddy Collins, went to the press after not being able to sleep for several days and speaking to Ricci's widow. Teddy, a crazy Irishman from Smith Hill, who lived right near we did and had gotten me and my father out of numerous jams over the years, stood in front of TV and newspaper reporters and stated Bob Ricci died because he would not lie.

Collins went on to say in detail that the Mayor was ramming unqualified men down Ricci's throat. Bob Ricci did not pull the trigger. Collins stated The System did. The Ricci tragedy highlighting politics and patronage in the city government was just the start of some dark days revisiting him from his law school days in Milwaukee, where he was involved in a rape and settlement to the victim of alleged rape.

The Providence Journal was hot on his trail. My family friend Teddy Collins was demoted to nights, and later was served a 3-year-old arrest warrant for code violations on some houses he owned in Smith Hill. Collins told the press this was retribution for standing up for Bob Ricci. Cianci dismissed Collins claims by saying no man is above the law, something he would find out all too well shortly.

No Shows

May 7, 1978 several guys were indicted in the scam involving the no show jobs at public works that we were given after the first election in 1975.

Several including my friend Billy (Blackjack) were arrested and suspended and another friend of mine Jacky Melvin, the City Highway superintendent, also had ties to mobsters. Melvin was on the job despite his arrest the prior year on unrelated charges of using a stolen credit card, kidnapping and beating a suspected mob informant with a wooden ax handle.

One of the other accused no shows had testified as an alibi witness the previous year at the trial of mobsters Jerry and Harold Tillinghast, for the execution of loan shark and our ex-friend George Basmajian.

My boss and close friend Anthony (Blackjack), an assistant highway superintendent and Cianci lieutenant, accused the Democrat attorney general of trying to smear us and Cianci. Blackjack's grand jury appearance had turned sour when the female prosecutor Susan McGurl started grilling him about alleged mob control of various Providence nightclubs. At that Time, he refused to answer any questions, because she was on a fishing expedition. Blackjack screamed at her that you are trying to frame people. I hang with a lot of wise guys and grew up on Federal Hill and what they do on the side is their business. Anthony then said, "I go to work every day and work for a living".

Several days later I was called in to testify before the same grand jury because two of the no-show employees were sidewalk inspectors in my department. In which I was the boss in charge of and gave out daily assignments for sidewalk inspections on a daily basis.

I testified that the two employees showed up every day and picked up their assignments, that I left for each of our six inspectors and was returned by the next morning completed. Billy "Blackjack" the older brother of Anthony, who was a Capo in the Patriarca Mob Family had been followed and caught selling suits out of his trunk. He was also followed leaving the city to drive to Boston to collect money for Patriarca.

At the end of my testimony the prosecutor said to me that you are one of the most professional liars she had ever questioned. I finished up by saying, "To the best of my knowledge they both do their work each day and I do not know anything about organized crime." I work two-three jobs to support my family, she asks how many are no-show jobs. None I responded. She then asked a question regarding the Cadillac I drove as a personal car and the ten gallons of gas the city allowed me to pump every day, which made me aware they were already following me.

I stayed away from Atwells Ave and the wise guys for a while so not to be brought back to court for perjury charges about the organized crime questions. My testimony helped Billy Blackjack get his job back with back pay and his pension.

Another Bulger Event

     A month later in July, I took a ride with a friend Billy "Black Jack" who was a Capo in the Patriarca family. Billy also worked with me for the City of Providence as a sidewalk inspector. We drove to South Boston to a garage where Billy was to collect money from Whitey Bulger, who paid kickbacks to the Office in Providence. I knew something was going to be said when he spots me with Billy.

     We arrived at this garage Billy goes in I stayed in auto which was a red convertible. Billy comes out after a minute followed by Bulger, and Bulger says to Billy, "Who's your sidekick? Yea I know him, you know from what I hear it's not safe up here in Boston for Irishmen they're finding them dead all over the place. There's a war going on up here you and your friends should keep your heads down and stay in Rhode Island.

I responded yeah, "I'll pass that along to all my friends including the Old Man meaning Patriarca, returning to Providence, I spoke to Kevin H. and my friends that did work for Patriarca and they were pissed. I did speak to Raymond the next day and his response was "Is that what the little prick said?" I said yes. Kevin also went to the old man and asked for permission to go to Boston to whack Bulger. Patriarca said no he is one of my best earners in New England. Raymond then said I will talk to the asshole about this shit and set him straight.

Looking into the future and the mob including the Patriarca crime family, it would have saved a lot of grief and lives because Bulger was the biggest rat in history because he ratted on everyone. Friends and foes, for over 30 years under the FBI protection. James J. "Whitey" Bulger was the infamous Irish Gangster from Boston.

He had become very famous in last few years because his 16 years on the run from FBI. He was America's most wanted criminal for all those years for being an FBI informant who they allowed him to kill at least 19 people.

Boston FBI agents allowed the murders because Bulger was informing on the Italian mafia, In New England including Patriarca's crime family. He now is serving 100's of years in federal prison in Plymouth, MA. Several FBI agents are doing life sentences also.

My Dad said when Bulger was on the run for all those years that someone should kill Bulgers brother Billy, because he was the only person Whitey cared about in this world. And that would make him suffer the pain he put so many other family's through.

Public Works Corruption

Most days I was the driver for "Buckles", who was the head of the highway department in public works for the City. Buckles was my sister's nephew through her marriage to Tony Bucci. Buckles was Tony's nephew and he was a very close associate to Buddy Cianci and Ronnie Glantz. When I was not driving "Buckles" I'd be driving Anthony "Blackjack" who was also a boss in public works who I was very close with, because we had worked together for several years before he became a boss. Anthony came from a family very well connected to the Patriarca mob family. On many day's we would stop in City Hall, head up to the Mayor's office were the gatekeeper would be. The gatekeeper was Ronnie

Glantz, who had a healthy respect for mob guys from his days as a city lawyer.

Several years earlier when he was assigned to a police case of a double murder at Pannone's market in Silver Lake. On this day bookies Rudy M. and Anthony M. were gunned down. Glantz said he had never seen a dead body before, and he remembered picking his way around the bullet riddled corpses in a state of shock. They had been shot with 12 gage shotguns.

Every time we would go up to Glantz office it was always a very jovial scene because when Blackjack, Buckles, and myself would arrive, always unannounced, we were allowed in and he would drop whatever he was doing or ask whoever he was with to leave. Blackjack was always teasing him that he would break his legs. On one of these visits Glantz was telling Blackjack that he wanted to get a Cadillac that his cousin Milton Berle was going to give him, but it was in Arizona. He needed to have someone drive it back to Providence and he asked Blackjack if he knew someone who would do it. His offer was to fly someone to Arizona and pay his way back for $500 dollars.

Blackjack then turned to me and said, "You want to do it, take the week off and fly down there?" I answered, "As long as I get paid to and not use my sick time I'll do it." And their answer was, of course.

Several days later I was flying to Arizona by myself. I had asked to have a friend come with me but Glantz said no he was tight with his money.
A limo driver met me in Phoenix, drives me to this big mansion out in the desert and escorts me inside. Several

people were having lunch and one is the famous Milton Berle who greets me and says, "So you're the driver of my Caddy huh kid?" I said yes sir and he goes on to tell me the history of this old Cady and what to do if I have problems with it on the long drive. He gave me a bunch of AAA maps for my return trip. He fed me lunch before I left for my trip back to Providence.

It took me five days and four nights to drive back to Providence. Upon my return, I drove up to the east side where Glantz lived and delivered the auto and keys to him that evening. Everyone was happy, and it just proved to everyone involved that I could be trusted with anything that needed to be done.

Mike Farina, a former real estate salesman, managed Cianci's 1974 and 1978 campaigns, he stayed on with Cianci after he took office to serve as his top political adviser. Cianci rewarded Farina by making him the Director of Public Property, a powerful department that oversaw city real estate, new construction and repairs to city buildings.

One flight up from the mayor's office was Farina office where he would throw parties for city contractors, one of those contractors was my friend Tommy R., Tommy had a silent partner, the partner was Buckles.

These parties produced butt-loads of booze, women and lots of wheeling and dealing. Guys would sit around and talk about various scams, padding contracts and billing for phantom work. Farina was eager to learn so he would pick people's brains like Tommy Ricci and Buckles, so he could understand how kickbacks worked.

I attended several of these meetings just for the food and the beer. Whoever I went with would tell me some of the stuff that was discussed that night.

Tommy R. wanted to be the main contractor for the city, so he wanted to get close to Farina. Tommy's company "Busy Bee Construction" built a second floor on Farina s Cranston home. Cianci had stopped by several of those gatherings and it made him angry and he fumed about the fact that all these contractors were treating Farina as if he was the King of Providence. This did not sit too well with Cianci.

Publicly Cianci continued to emphasize that he was running a clean city government, but really it was a cesspool, everything and anything was for sale at the right price.

Behind the scene Cianci would tell Ricci and Buckles he wanted to fire Farina but did not have the votes on the city council to fire department heads without council approval.

The war started when Cianci tried to reassign Farina's purchasing power, to a deputy who had sold $10,000 worth of tickets for Cianci's fund to city vender's and bypassing Farina. Farina struck back and called a Providence Journal reporter and detailed how a particular deputy had often had split up purchases from a chemical company with ties to Cianci.

This was a way to circumvent the competitive bidding requirement for purchases of $1500.00 or more. The reporter found that Custom Chemical had a partner who was married to Cianci's cousin, Custom Chemical seen their city business triple to $250.000 in the Mayor's first two years.

Buckles told me he considered the split between Cianci and Farina a falling out of two thieves. Farina had gotten too greedy, but the last straw was that Farina learned that Cianci had Ronnie Glantz slip into Public Property Office, on a weekend and steamed open envelopes containing sealed bids for a large trash contract.

This was done to rig the bid for a company paying kickbacks to Farina. After this event Farina told Cianci that if he got the votes on the council to fire him, he would then make a speech against Cianci on the courthouse steps. Cianci then turned up the heat on Farina. One day I was with Buckles, and Anthony Blackjack, I was driving near the state house when we got a call to go to city hall and see Ronnie Glantz.

We went upstairs and Glantz met us and brought us in his back office. He said Farina is a rat and we must stop the bastard from opening his big mouth to the Journal or worse the Feds. He gave Buckles and Blackjack a mission to follow Farina, show up at his office every day to just say hello and when following him make sure he sees that you around there. Hopefully this will put the fear of God into the prick, and he will just go away soon when he is fired.

Every day for a week or so I would drive Blackjack to city hall where we would go to Farina office and sit in an outer office till he came out to let him know we were there and make small talk. We would leave and then return later when Farina would leave city hall. A secretary in the lobby would call dispatch at public works to let us know where he was going. we would then make another visual contact with him. Were we would exchange waves and he finally got the message. Cianci finally got the votes to oust Farina, so he left city hall quietly and there were no speeches on the courthouse steps or elsewhere.

This was another example of where the power in Providence lied, not with Cianci so much, but the fear of the mob and Raymond Patriarca who was the real power broker in RI.

Sean Collins

Show Biz

I was always hustling to make money and would work as an extra in any Movie or TV shows that would film in RI. The fact that I worked for the city which allowed me to make my own hours. I worked on The Way We Were, The Great Gadsby, 3 Days of The Condor to name a few.

I attended a wedding in Warwick RI in February of 1980, when a woman came up to me and introduced herself as Donna Del Santo. She was the owner of Rhode Island Model Agency in Warwick. She asked me if I had ever thought about modeling and acting because she thought I was a very attractive man, and I looked like a professional athlete. I responded yes but was working two-three jobs and always looking to make more money. She then asked me to come to her studio in Warwick for some photos she thought she had a project that I was perfect for.

I went in soon after the wedding and had the photos taken and many were of me shirtless. The project she had in mind was a Lifebuoy Soap TV commercial in NYC in two weeks with the Ford Agency. I was chosen for the National Commercial as a baseball player, then in a shower bare-chested. The commercial paid $13,000 and residuals. I did the National Commercial under the name of John Francis Sullivan which qualified me to be a member of AFTRA TV Union.

Many years later in 2006 while living in Florida I received a call from a friend in Rhode Island that several TV and film projects were being shot in RI because of the tax incentives being giving out by the state. My friend had known that I had worked on numerous film projects in the 1970s and 1980s.

At the time, I was retired living on a golf course and was interested in making some money and this was a way to get back in the film business, so I went back to Rhode Island and was casted in the first project I read for. Waterfront was a CBS TV show they were filming in Providence and I was cast as a Union Officer who did not get along with the Mayor the lead character of the series

From there it was the Feature Film the Game Plan, 21, Dan In Real Life, Evenings, and Brotherhood a Showtime series about the Irish mob in Providence. I was an Italian Gangster and Stunt Fighter. On this project, I earned my SAG Union Card, but had to change my stage name to Sean Collins because there had been 23 John Sullivan's that were SAG members over the years. This allowed me to work in NYC and Los Angeles or any other region of the country on SAG Union projects.

So, for the last ten years I have worked and lived in LA and NYC working on many projects mostly as a Mobster. Bad guy roles on TV including Heroes, Sons of Anarchy, Knight Rider, Law and Order, Criminal Minds, and Blue Bloods to name a few.

Family Drama

When I think back and remember my grandmother, I think of her as a saint. She helped raise about eight of her grandchildren, myself and my sister Margie full time, Bobby and Billy Corry, and Eddie Bannon. All of which were children by her daughters. Billy Corry and his older brother Bobby were like brothers to me. Billy was one year older than me, Bobby three years older. They were always at my grandmothers during the day and would go home at night to sleep.

Bobby Corry was like a big brother to me and all my cousins, he was one of the nicest people that was ever a part in my life. He was a kind and caring and a very respectful person. Bobby was too nice it seemed to be part of my crazy family, so he was always trying to keep us out of trouble.

One-time Bobby had trouble with a gang of tough guys from Pawtucket who had bothered him and his wife at a softball game. Bobby was too nice and the type to turn the other cheek and just walk away. This time Bobby asked a few of us to go to Pawtucket and talk too these guys so it would not happen again, because Bobby enjoyed playing softball in Pawtucket, and he purchased a home in the area. Well we piled into two autos, there were eight to ten of us, with bats and clubs because we never went anywhere to talk things out. We pulled up to this parking area in the park where there was a crowd of guys milling about behind a backstop.

My cousin Bobby got out of his auto, when of the assholes yelled to him calling him a pussy. Saying what are you guys going to do. He was the biggest guy there, I guess he was the ringleader. His gang stood in a line opposite to where we were acting big and bad. I was probably the youngest guy there and one the smallest, but I was known to have more balls than brains at times, I ran ahead of my group right at the big mouth leader with a baseball bat in my hand and before he could move I smacked him right in the head. I dropped him in a flash, his head was covered in blood. One other guy in that group responded to me when he did I cracked him right in the side of the head sending him flying to the ground. My actions shocked both sides and the fight was over right then. Everyone was saying they were sorry to my cousin Bobby and no one ever bothered him again. I remember Bobby just looking at me with a big smile on his face shaking his head saying, "You are just like your father, you are something else."

It was several years later when I experienced one of the worse days of my life. It was Labor Day weekend and my softball team, The City of Providence, was playing in the New England Championships at Gano Street in Providence. We had been undefeated all year and had won the State of RI title and now Bobby had spent the weekend watching my team win and have the right to go to the US National Championship in Texas.

Well on September 2,1978, Bobby left my side at Gano Street Park, to go play in a charity softball game. In the second inning, Bobby got a hit and was on first base, the next batter hit the ball that required Bobby to run to second and he was struck by the thrown ball by the second baseman in the center of his chest. Closing his aorta for just three minutes and he died on the field after numerous people trying to resuscitate him. By the Time I returned home from my own game and short celebration I received a call that Bobby had passed away, I was stunned and dropped to my knees in my home crying like a baby.

Several of my other cousins died very young way before there times, Kevin, Joey, and Maryann Randell died in their 40s. Along with my closest cousin Billy Corry all by drinking and drug addictions.

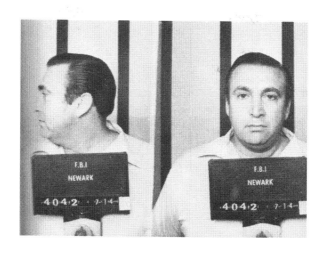

Roy DeMeo

During the early 80s, my friends and I would sell hot stolen autos. We would get two kids to steal autos over state line in Massachusetts at the Showcase Theater in Seekonk and pay them $50. They stole autos that were very precise models, new luxury autos for the most part. We would buy a set of VIN plates on the motors and doors; the VIN plates usually were a set of five plates from a junkyard dealer. We generally paid $100 for a set of plates. We usually would steal the same type of vehicle, replace the numbers and sell them as new and legal autos. We earned a lot of money and we all drove these auto's ourselves for years.

My Dad found out what we were doing with these hot cars, he suggested to get in contact with a longtime friend of his from NYC. The contact was with the mastermind of the biggest auto theft ring in New York history. The guy's name was Roy DeMeo, besides being a car thief, he was also one of the most feared hitman in the city for John Gotti and the Gambino Family, with more than 200 brutal slayings attributed to him and his crew.

Dad had hooked me up with Roy and the hot car business, we would grab the cars in New England and drive them to a junkyard outside of NYC and be paid cash for cars that were being shipped out of the country to the middle east. Most of the autos were Caddy's and Lincolns. Dad told me to have as little contact with Roy as possible because he was a scary guy, and if I ever had issues about money with Roy let him know and he would take care of it.

Tragic story Roy met his demise because of the stolen autos and not all the murders he did. He was found in the trunk of his Caddy. Shot numerous times and his body was frozen from being in the trunk for five days in sub-zero temperatures

Providence Civic Center

     I had worked at the Providence Civic Center since 1972 when it first opened as a security guard and a stage hand from time to time. In November 1981, my cousin Billy was running for Union Business Manager of the International Alliance of Theatrical Stage Employees (IATSE). IATSE is the surname of the Union in Providence RI.

     A week before the election, Billy called me and asked me to meet him at the Civic Center, which I did later that day and he told me he was having problems with some of the members and that they would not support anyone besides the current business manager who was running for re-election. Billy asked me if I would do something to put the fear of God in his opponent before the election and help him win. The night before the election there was an event at the civic center where I was working as a security guard in uniform. As I was leaving that evening, I was walking in the rear parking lot with several of my fellow security guards, one was named Brendon, who would later become Chief of the State Police in RI and the other friend was Eddy Mac who later became an FBI agent. Back to that evening I went to my auto and pulled out a 12-gage shotgun and proceeded to an auto that belong to my cousin Billy's opponent in the election.

I blew out the side and front windows of his Cadillac in full view of my friends, the other security guards. I proceeded to my auto put the gun away and drove off to Eddy Mac house where we shared a case of beer in next two hours. At no time did either Brendon or Eddy ask me about what had occurred, or why I did what I did, and I never offered any explanation.

The next day was the election and there was a lot of buzz about the auto shooting. My cousin won the election by 27 votes. A week or so later some FBI agents came to public works to talk to me about a possible RICO charge regarding the interference in the election process. They took me to the Court House and put me in a room. I stated that I wanted my attorney and never answered a question and was let go. They questioned Billy and he did the same thing. Before long the case was closed. Billy went on to be the Business Manager for close to 20 years until his death at age 46.

Billy Corry put hundreds of guys and gals to work at the Providence Civic Center and PPAC and several other venues. Billy was one of the most respected and loved person to ever grow up in Providence. He was like a brother to me and he was my Hero.

1982 BUSY YEAR

1982 was the busiest year I can ever remember especially for a City worker who was used to be a no-show employee. I was used to making my own hours to work at the civic center or as an extra in a film project or my weekend job at Foxy Lady's or Club Fantasy as a Doorman/Bouncer both places were owned by wise guys. The downside was that I very seldom got to spend time with my children Jay and Kelly.

I was being followed by the Feds most days who were trying get evidence of corruption against all of us at public works. Private contractors like Frank "Bobo" M. and Tommy R. where being watched also. They were close friends with Buckles and Anthony "Blackjack", who was responsible for paving roads and replacing sidewalks for the city.

In February Buckles and Blackjack were called to a meeting at city hall with Cianci and Ronnie Glantz, the

Mayor's bagman among other duties he performed in the most corrupt city government known to mankind. At this meeting, it was discussed how to get Cianci elected in November as an Independent instead of Republican as he had been in the past. During this meeting, the group came up with the motto of "Democrats for Cianci", a political action committee of sorts. Buckles and Blackjack were told to come up with a plan to sway votes Cianci's way with the fence sitters in Mt Pleasant, East Side, and the North End sections of Providence. Where most people always voted Democratic. They were also told that the city was launching the most ambitious public works program in history, a $2.9 million blitz to repave streets and repair sidewalks. They wanted us to repave one hundred streets, and one thousand sidewalks in those areas of the city that those voters lived in as a way of buying votes.

I was given a job of looking through the voting books to write down possible addresses of people who may be swayed Cianci's way if they were given a new sidewalk. Or paved their street in front of their home. I looked at their party affiliation regarding voting in the past. And I would send out sidewalk inspectors with picks and sledge hammer to inspect property that needed to be repaired. William "Blackjack" the Capo in Patriarca crime family was one of my inspectors. Cianci's political opponents accused him of buying votes. We just said the city was addressing the backlog of complaints dating back to 1964. The program offered Cianci's people unlimited opportunities for graft and kickbacks. Santi Campanella was a buddy of Cianci and given the contract to pave the streets in the city. Campanella had been partners with Raymond Patriarca, and Frank Sinatra in the Berkshire Downs racetrack in the 70s.

Meanwhile back at public works, I was filling out applications for every sidewalk that was repaired. I filled out and signed 430 applications. My catholic school training came in hand with being able to write with both hands. The nuns used to crack my left hand with their rulers because they used to say it was the devil's way, we were forced to learn how to write with both hands.

That started the steering of seven thousand tons of asphalt by Buckles, to Bobo M's paving company which he would use on private projects. It was said to be worth $150,000 in asphalt, many times Buckles would tell me to go asphalt plant in my city car and stand there and give the signal to plant operator, by touching of my belt buckle which was the signal to bill the city and fill up the truck with asphalt to be used at private jobs.

My daughter and I were out on a Sunday afternoon in May of 1982 taking a ride in my auto and we were driving on Jewett St in the Smith Hill section of Providence. As we were driving we heard a very loud bang in rear of my auto and it shocked us, so I pulled over to check what had occurred. When I got out and looked inside trunk area there was a dent on the back-panel driver's side. I spotted a softball in the street and a guy running down driveway to retrieve the ball. I called out to him and said, "Hey your ball put dent in my car". He said, "SO!!! What do I give a fuck!!?" I said, "Who the fuck you're talking too?" So right then a second guy comes down driveway with baseball bat and he's giving me shit to Saying fuck you. My daughter Kelly is in my car and she starts crying Daddy, Daddy Watch out!! Another guy comes down driveway with tire iron in his hand. They are yelling fuck you, get out of here before we kick your ass, my daughter is screaming by this point.

I tell the three guys stay right here I'll be right back, I drive my daughter to her home which is right around the corner and bring her inside to her mother. I jumped back in my car and race back to scene of the incident with three guys. I grabbed the 32 pistol I had under my seat and jump out of car. There are only two guys out there now I jumped out like a Wildman saying, "What are you going to do to me now assholes", as I pistol whip one of them on side of head dropping him and repeat the same to the other guy with a whack to the temple he goes down, now the 3rd guy comes running out with his tire iron like he is going to hit me, I raised the gun pointed it at his head and said, "Come on mother fucker" and walked forward to put it right on his forehead, he drops the tire iron, it clangs to the ground. I then grab the guy by the shirt and put the pistol in his mouth and say, "Now what are you guys going to do to me!" Everyone is screaming from the house, So I ask the guy with gun in his mouth what you going to do, that's when I realized the guy was pissing himself onto the ground in silence.

Everyone's yelling for the cops, so I just punched the last guy right in the face knocking him down, then go back to my car and leave before cops show up. I left the scene and drove to my apartment on Smith Street near the State House. I go upstairs with the pistol and lay down and take a nap for hour. When I wake from my nap I look outside from my second-floor apartment and discovered my auto was gone. I rush downstairs and someone tells me the cops towed my car away to the station.

I called police station and inquired about my car and they referred me to Det. Donald, a childhood friend of mine and who happened to be a cop. He tells me to come down to station he needs to talk to me. I went downtown to see him, and he asked me what happened so for first time in my life I am talking to a cop. I tell the story and he said he would do same thing if it happened to him, but his bosses want to know what the rubber gloves and box of bullets under the seat are all about? They want to know if I was working with my father on jobs whacking people because of the rubber gloves they were freaking out. I just gave some lame excuse to Donald, I was very lucky that Donald was working that Sunday afternoon because he swept it under the rug. He gave me my keys to my car and just said stay away from the area of Jewett St.

Well to my surprise the next morning, the incident is front page Providence Journal stating Smith Hill man pistol whips three and leaves scene. I was never ID in newspaper and never charged in the case. I was always lucky knowing people in power on both sides to the law. One day in late May of 1982, I had a fistfight on Atwells Ave near The Office of Raymond Patriarca with a wise guy named James Romano. I beat the shit out of the guy and the fight was broken up by Nicky Bianco. This fight started a big argument on the hill because an Irish kid kicking shit of an Italian. Patriarca called me up to his office and asked me what happened, I told him, and he said don't worry about it the guy was wrong. Romano was angry when he finds out he can't do anything to me.

A few months later he breaks into the house of a girl I was seeing to scare her and find out where I am staying. A few days later   Romano is in a bar with my friend Jimmy Martin and makes statement that I do not know how to take care of my woman. Jimmy just nods and calls me at home short time later and tells me the story figures Romano must be the guy that scared my friend. Jimmy tells me the guy is leaving town soon and he will take care of it.

The next night I get a call from Jimmy and he said I've taken care of it! talk soon. I turn the TV on at 11pm and the first story is about a killing that took place at Vincent's Restaurant. Romano was shot and killed while having dinner with his brother on Atwells Ave that night. A man walked in wearing a mask and dark clothing wearing gloves, the man came in the side door and walked up to the table were Romano was dining with his brother and shot Romano twice in the head, and quickly ran out.

I spoke with Jimmy a few days later he told me the cops had questioned him regarding the killing and they believe he was the killer but could not find a motive. I said thank you gave him a hug and we never spoke about it again.

In August of 1982, Bobo M. had problems when drag racing Billy Ferl another mobster on their bikes. He was cut off by a VW driven by Ronald McElroy, a 20-year-old kid on Westminster St. Bobo beat the kid to death with a baseball bat and he later was charged with murder but was acquitted because no one would testify against Frank because of fear.

Also, in 1982 Frank was charged with the murder of Anthony 'The Moron' Mirabella when he cornered him at Fida's Restaurant on Valley St in Providence. As the restaurant was closing after 1 am Bobo shot and then stabbed Moron and dragged him into back kitchen with the owner in fear of getting wacked himself. Mirabella was just released from prison for a double murder at a liquor store up on Broadway. Mirabella had walked in and shot the owner and one customer to death with a shotgun in a robbery.

In 1982 Cianci's administration was being shaken down by the Laborers Union. A rally led by President Arthur Coia Sr went to City Hall to protest pension issues. Coia who answered personally to the Mob and Raymond Patriarca, told Cianci that if he wanted to win in November he would have to raise the city contribution to the union's pension, and to the union's legal defense fund.

Which he did because nothing moved in Providence without Coia's okay and Patriarca permission. Cianci won the election by 1000 votes with 42% of the vote.

Another tragic event took place down in Smith Hill one Friday night. A bunch of us guys were drinking at Smith Hill Tap on Smith Street, playing poker and pool and anything to pass the time waiting for last call at midnight most of the time. After last call, everyone would go some were else to have a couple more drinks, we all were professional drinkers on Smith Hill or, so we thought.

One of my friends named Kevin L. left the tap and walked around the corner to Harry's Tap on Chalkstone Ave. Kevin went inside and they were closing also there were three men inside Harry's. Kevin had some sort of incident in there about getting another drink, well Kevin pulled his handgun out and shot all three guys. Two died right there and the 3rd survived with severe wounds. This was another example where violence played itself out in our neighborhood. Kevin was arrested charged with the two murders and spent the rest of his days at the ACI in Cranston.

Some Personal Issues

Around February 1983, I went to my ex-wife's house to return a small portable TV to my son that I had borrowed from him. We were divorced in 1980 and there were times that I went by her house to pick up the kids or drop something off to my three children. I was driving my city car with a fellow worker Mike Jennings as a passenger, I walked up to the 3rd floor where they lived and knocked on the door and my son opened the door and was excited to see me. As he opened the door I seen a man run in the background naked to the bathroom. Something in me snapped because I went into the apartment before I knew it my ex-wife's boyfriend was standing face to face and he was yelling something at me, so I struck him with a left-handed backhand in the face which I learned later broke his nose and cheek because I had to pay for the plastic surgeon to fix his face as ordered by the court. After the slap, I grabbed him and pushed his ass through the window in the kitchen almost pushing him out the 3rd floor window. At this point my ex-wife jumped on my back to stop me from throwing him to the street. She was yelling and that brought me back to reality and I stopped. I walked down the stairs to go out and I was met by two Providence cops who attempted to handcuff me and that did not go well. I was told by my fellow worker Mike afterwards that I was throwing the cops off me like rag dolls, and so they both struck me in the head several times until both called their boss who was a friend of mine, Lt Billy Campbell showed up and got me to stop.

I was arrested and taken down to the station to be processed on three counts of simple assault; one on the boyfriend and two on police officers because they broke the clubs over my head. They were covering themselves against me suing them for excessive force. The Officer in charge at the police station was Lt Teddy Collins a family friend and he took care of me. He asked me if I was working when this occurred, I said yes, he then asked who is your lawyer, "I said Arthur Coia Jr." He then told me to get out of here before you get fired and I'll call your lawyer for you to be in court in the morning. My ex-wife and her boyfriend were furious when they arrived to press charges because I had already been released and back to work in a half hour. I was at my arrangement the next morning with my lawyer and told to come back in a month. When we returned to court for my first hearing my lawyer said follow me as we looked in several courtrooms to see what Judge was on the bench until we found Judge DeSantis courtroom and we went in and Arthur asked for a sidebar with the Judge and then came back to me nodding his head saying Ok we are good.

The Judge calls me up and says to me, "Losing your temper again John and I see that you have a hard head breaking nightsticks on the cops huh", I said, "Yes sir, I lost my cool." He stated that he agrees with Arthur that this case should be filed with a no-lo pleading to the charges for one year, if I pay medical bill for the boyfriend and court costs. I said thank you sir, he responded be good for a year and this thing did not happen. I smiled and said yes sir. This how justice works in RI if you know the right people or they know you.

Feds Are Watching

We at Public works were aware of we were being watched and trailed by the Feds and that they were listening devices in our offices trying to get evidence against "Buckles" and "Blackjack". They were their main targets for the corruption. All the important conversations that needed to be discussed where made outside of our building or in a the very loud truck garage.

In March 1983, The Providence police was investigating Public Works employees who they said collected paychecks but do not work. And Mayor Cianci covering his own ass by requested the investigation, The Providence Journal reported that 18 of the department 120 employees are no-shows. One of them, Anthony B. was my brother-in-law and whom I lived with on Federal Hill at the time.

Chief of Providence Police Anthony Mancuso called in the press and Federal and State Law

Enforcement officials and City Council Members. Mancuso displayed two lists one of Public Works employees with criminal records, the other of Public Works employees with ties to organized crime. The Providence Journal reported that my name was on both lists. It then went on to talk about corruption in other departments, no-show jobs, bid rigging, payoffs for jobs, promotions, and city contracts. Seven Public Works Employees were indicted by the state in the no show jobs scam. My brother-in-law, Anthony B. was one of those charged. Another official indicted was Jack M, another friend of mine, who was the night Highway Superintendent. Jackie was charged with kidnapping and participating in the beating of a suspected mob informant with a wooden ax handle. Jacky joined Buckles and Blackjack in calling the charges false and a frame up by Law Enforcement.

I was called before several grand jury hearings into all the corruption charges and was always given immunity because as they knew I went to work every day and was the smartest one in public works. I testified for my Brother-in law, that I dropped him off at Public Works every night where he was a night security officer after picking him up at his Pizza Shop in Fox Point. They did not believe me, and Tony was convicted and given probation.

"Buckles" The Highway Superintendent was indicted in Federal Court on April 22, 1984. The grand jury charged him with extortion of $64,000 in kickbacks from three snow removal contractors two of whom never provided any service to the city. They also had questions about the snow removal from previous year's budgets. It had gone up from $480.000 to $1.2 Million in 1983.

I was called as a witness at his grand jury hearing and his trial in which half way through it Buckles took a plea deal for 48 months in federal prison. I also gave testimony at Billy Blackjacks trial for being a no show and he was acquitted because I testified he came in every day and his work was completed each day and was awarded all his back pay for 18 months. And Billy paid it forward when my brother-in-law, Tony had a stroke and was in a Boston Hospital in danger of dying. I asked Billy if he had some extra money for my sister and her children for Christmas and on December 23rd, he sees me on Atwells Ave and calls me over and hands me $500 for my sister and says if she needs more come see him, another example of a great guy with bad reputation.

"Buddy" **Cianci** for Mayor
The Anti-Corruption Candidate

Cianci's Downfall

On March 8, 1983, Cianci called a contractor named Raymond DeLeo to his home on Power St. Because he believed DeLeo was having an affair with his ex-wife. When DeLeo arrived Cianci instructed his police bodyguard to frisk DeLeo. DeLeo screamed "What the hell is this?" There were two other men in the room watching the event unfold, Joseph DiSanto, and William McNair.

Cianci came over to DeLeo and accused him of screwing his wife. Cianci began hitting DeLeo in the head. Cianci continued to hit DeLeo and dared him to hit him back. Cianci told DeLeo that Judge McNair had some papers for him to sign which was a confession that he had been sleeping with Sheila. There was also a contract that DeLeo would pay Cianci $500,000 for having the affair, Cianci continued to hit DeLeo and vowed to ruin his business. Cianci was a crazed man, his eyes were bloodshot, and snot was running from his nose. It was like something had snapped in him. Cianci's rage escalated and he threw liquor on DeLeo, spit on him and even tried to put out his lit cigarette in DeLeo's left eye.

Cianci became further enraged and grabbed a log from the fireplace and raised it over DeLeo's head. DiSanto rushed over and helped DeLeo block the blow. Cianci was in the kitchen when McGair called Herbert DeSimone. They figured DeSimone's powerful presence could end this horrific event. DeSimone arrived at about 10:30 pm and couldn't believe the scene. Cianci's wild look and the battered body of DeLeo He asked Cianci, "What's happening here?" Cianci told DeSimone that DeLeo had been having an affair with his ex-wife. Cianci went to hit DeLeo again but DeSimone put Cianci in a bear hug and took him into the kitchen. While there, DiSanto told DeLeo to get out of there as fast as he could. DeLeo later testified he wouldn't leave because the policeman was between him and the door. DeLeo was to deliver a certified check for $500,000 to Cianci by Friday, or he'd be dead. "He reiterated to DeLeo that he must understand the terms. DeLeo responded, "Yes, I understand.". They then allowed DeLeo to leave. DeLeo called the State Police the next day to file charges against Cianci.

Days after the altercation with Cianci, DeLeo experienced headaches was treated by a neurosurgeon for injuries to his face and head to include the burn marks to his left eye that Cianci inflicted on him with his cigarette.

During a grand jury hearing, DeSanto remembered Cianci threatening to ruin DeLeo's business, shouting, crying, and acting irrationally. De Santo said he didn't hear the Cianci tell DeLeo that he would be "dead" if he didn't come up with the $500,000. On May 24, 1983, A RI Grand Jury Indicted Buddy Cianci on charges of conspiracy, kidnapping, assault, assault with a deadly weapon, and attempted extortion. Cianci's police bodyguard James Hassett, was also indicted on charges of kidnapping and conspiracy to kidnap.

On April 23,1984, Cianci was convicted of all charges, he received a five-year suspended sentence. Which made him a convicted felon. The following day Buddy Cianci resigned as Mayor of Providence, this was required by the Providence City Charter. This was not the last of Buddy Cianci's career as Mayor of the City of Providence. He would return after serving the suspended sentence. He was re-elected Mayor several times and did a great job rebuilding downtown Providence. Until corruption issues came up again, this time he was sent to Federal Prison.

Legal Trouble in Providence

In Dec 1983, Raymond Patriarca was charged with the murder of Raymond Baby Curio who was killed in 1965 for burglarizing the home Raymond's brother's.

On March 13, 1984, Raymond was arrested while in the hospital for ordering the murder of Bobby Candos who was about to testify against Raymond for the 1965 murder of Curio. "Buckles" The Highway Superintendent and my cousin was indicted in Federal Court on April 22, 1984. The grand jury charged him with extortion of $64,000 in kickbacks from three snow removal contractors two of whom never provided any service to the city. They also had questions about the snow removal from previous year's budgets. It had gone up from $480.000 to $1.2 Million in 1983.

I was called as a witness at his grand jury hearing and his trial in which half way through it Buckles took a plea deal for 48 months in Federal prison. I also gave testimony at Billy Blackjacks trial for being a no show and he was acquitted because I testified he came in every day and his work was completed each day and was awarded all his back pay for 18 months.

On April 23, 1984, the Mayor received a 5-year suspended prison sentence, which made him a convicted felon. On April 25, 1984, Buddy Cianci resigned as Mayor of Providence according to the Providence City Charter which required him to do so. Council President Joseph Paolino from Federal Hill a young guy born with a silver spoon in his mouth and whose family owned millions in real estate around the city was sworn in as Mayor of Providence. I was one of the few leftovers in public works because I never gave up my union membership even though I was working in executive positions over the last few years I had the title of Sidewalk Inspector and Inspector in Environmental Control.

On July 11, 1984 Raymond Patriarca suffered a heart attack at the home of his girlfriend and passed away, he was 76 years old and had been out on bail when he died because of his health. Raymond was waked at Berarducci Funeral home on Broadway in Providence and buried in the Gates of Heaven Cemetery.

Taking Care Business

In 1966 a group of men were playing cards at a social club on Federal St in the Federal Hill section. These were a group of guys that knew each other from childhood and were Italians who had the ok from Raymond Patriarca to have the card game and was under his protection against anyone who was crazy idea to rob the game or for the police to show up for a sting

There were a group of 10 guys in the club drinking very heavy and it was getting near midnight and last call was called and just a few more hands of poker were to be played.

One guy named Smitty was bombed and started a big argument about last call and the card game being over because he was losing. Smitty started yelling at the bartender and his friend named "John Bono" who was sitting with his back to the bar when Buffy pulled out a pistol and shot John in the back killing him right there in his chair. Smitty was subdued and arrested by Providence Police right on the scene. John Bono was my brother in law's older brother. Tony is who I lived with after my grandmother died and was also my best man at my second marriage.

Smitty was found guilty of murder and put away in state prison for 20yrs, He did his time and was released in 1984. When he hit the streets, he had a lot of bravado because he was not killed in prison after killing an associate of the Patriarca Crime Family.

Well no sooner than Smitty got out of prison he started telling anyone that would listen that he was going to take care of the rest of the Bono family. Well word spread fast and a decision was made after three weeks that this guy had a death wish and had to go quick fast.

So, the plan was set in motion, Smitty had a family social club that he was in every night up in Silver Lake, and always on Friday and Saturday nights. This social club had an old-style phone booth near the front door away from the bar and pool tables and card tables. Well on this summer Friday night a call was placed to that phone booth and Smitty answered the phone and was told that they had a message from the Bono family. He was told that the callers voice was the last voice he would ever hear. Smitty said, "Fuck the Bonos's" the caller then heard two shotgun blasts that killed Smitty instantly. No one was ever charged in this murder.

Club Fantasy

I met my second wife, Maryellen at the Club Fantasy. I was working a second job as a Doorman/ Bouncer at a Strip Club called Fantasy, Maryellen was Bartending there. It was her second job. We dated for eight months then moved in together for a few months before we got married on May 31, 1985. By getting married we now had a combined family of seven. My three children and her two, it was not easy by any means combining all these kids, all were jealous of the others.

I was working at my children's school picnic at St. Ann's on Atwells Ave on a Sunday afternoon, many local politicians show their faces at these events to try to get votes. I was working one of the food tables when the new mayor of Providence Joe Paolino comes up to the table I was working, Paolino knew me from Federal Hill and that I was related his enemy Buckles. He also knew I was a boss down at Public Works working on cleaning dirty lots in South Providence. Paolino then asks me how the lot cleaning was going, I replied very well, we have cleaned up 65 lots so far. But if we had some more supplies we could wrap the project earlier than planned. Well I guess he did not like my response and his aide wrote something in his little pad.

Well the next morning I arrived at Public Works to start my shift, my boss calls me into his office and asks me what I had said to Paolino yesterday. I responded that I answered his question.

Well he said you embarrassed him in front of others. And he wants you in the south side of the city cleaning lots by yourself. I said tell that prick to go "Fuck Himself". I knew he was going to come after me at some point, but I was going to beat him to the punch. I was still a union member and a steward, so he could not just fire me as he could other managers. But I had a plan because I knew how to work the system better than most because I saved many union workers over the years as a steward. It is very difficult to fire someone who is in the mental health or drug and alcohol program. I went upstairs to the director Frank T. who I had something on, regarding him allowing Bobo M. to do some private asphalt work for him with city asphalt. This was something Buckles had taught many years ago, to watch everyone because everyone is crooked, and everyone has a price they will pay to save their ass or pension. I just asked Frank if he remembered the event and he asked me what I needed, and I responded that I was going to put myself in a place called High Point, a drug and mental health program that was 28 days long and I only had 20 sick days and needed what they called a sick leave extension. Frank said ok I will give you a 90day extension on your sick leave to take care of your family.

So, a few days later I checked in for a 28-day substance abuse program which was a breeze because I was just a social user of speed and sleeping pills. Well in High point one day I was angry about a phone call from someone on the outside and I punched a metal door and my right hand exploded I had a compound fracture the bone came right through the skin and severed some nerves in my hand. A pin was implanted in my right hand for eight weeks. When I was released from High Point I stayed home several weeks for the hand to heal or at least have the pin removed it still was not healing well.

It was early winter when I came back to public works and was riding shotgun in a snow plow truck and it was sleeting rain when I slipped while getting out of the 10-wheel truck fell on sidewalk on my right hand injuring it again. I went hospital and they said my hand was fractured and I needed surgery and a fusion and pin in my hand again. Since I was injured at work I went on Workers Comp and was given 66% per cent of my pay tax free. I collected workers comp for over a year. During this time, I started taking college classes at Johnson and Wales and Roger Williams College I was taking Pre-Law Classes and did an Internship in the Public Defender's Office. During this time, I was able to expunge all my past criminal records.

After the Second surgery and losing feeling in my little finger in my right hand I put in for a disability pension because I knew my career was over with the city of Providence because they know had time clocks and all sorts of other things to watch employees and that was not for me. To receive a disability pension, you must go to three doctors. It is not an easy thing to get approved especially at 34 years old. When I visited the Doctors they all new I injured my hand badly and asked me if given a pension what was I going to do with my life from this point on, I answered that I was taking law classes which I was and that I wanted to be a professional lawyer like they were professional doctors, doctors and lawyers have this thing that they are better than others and I fit right into their ego by wanting to be one of them. As far as I know all three doctors gave me the ok. And the city retirement board approved my pension five to one, the one no was Mayor Joseph Paolino. I was also told that I was given the pension to shut my mouth and get out of town, which was my plan anyways.

During the process of waiting for the pension to go through I had taken a job as a baggage handler in Boston at Logan airport. I had to work six months there before I could transfer to somewhere in Florida, soon after I took a transfer to Tampa. Where could I start a new life. "Out of Sight Out of Mind" was my motto because I always felt that I would have taken a bullet in the head, for all the dirty stuff I knew about. Or someone wanting to get back at my father or being ratted on for working as a baggage handler with my pension because most went to jail around me a Public

Works and lost everything and I walked away with a pension and health insurance for life.

The Plan that I had thought through for several years to allow me to get away from world of mobsters and all that goes with it and the political world all came together. When I received my pension from the City of Providence in 1986, I was given several large settlements for injuries and the 90 sick days. I was entitled to settlement for scars on my hand and a worker's comp settlement from the city of Providence along with $1200 a month plus blue cross for life, I could not of ask for more.

New Life in Florida

In March of 1989, I moved to Dunedin, Florida, and worked for American Airlines in Tampa. I was working for American Airlines in Providence and I took a transfer as soon as possible to get out of sight of anyone in Rhode Island.

My wife and children moved to Tampa in July of 1989 and we purchased a home right on a canal on the Gulf of Mexico for $65,000 which was unheard of in New England. Maryellen and I were starting a new life away from all the craziness of Providence, left behind for the most part. Although having flying benefits which allowed us to fly anywhere we chose to we returned to Providence four or five times a year to see her family and for me to visit my Father who really settled down and was working a real job, at the Providence Journal as the midnight security guard and resident bookie. The place was full of gamblers and he loved them, and they loved him. He worked there from 1989 to 2001, until he got ill with cancer again. Dad retired reluctantly. He would have worked until he died because he hated staying home and doing nothing. He went through bouts of cancer going into remission for short time in 2001. My father and I talked on the phone at least once a week, he would keep me in touch with everything going on in New England crime world and political goings on with Buddy Cianci. Who was re-elected in January of 1991, after spending several years as the Top-Rated Radio Talk show host in RI. Cianci second term was much more productive than his first term and he was credited with bring the city back to life and creating a downtown that brought over 100,000 people to the city each summer, in 1998 ran unopposed for reelection.

When I think of the mob in Rhode Island, I am reminded of Raymond Patriarca Jr. He was a very weak leader and was taped conducting a mob induction ceremony in Boston in which he and eight other mobsters were put in prison for nine yrs.

My former friend Nicky Bianco was arrested and convicted of conspiracy to murder in 1991 and sentenced to 11 years, but he passed away in 1994 from ALS in Federal prison. In 1992 Kevin H. was shot and killed by two men on Atwells Ave, not two blocks from where the Romano killing took place ten years earlier. I have personally carried a lot of guilt around inside for many years now because my actions or reactions have caused a chain of events that have taken people's lives or changed them forever.

My childhood friend Gerry T. was released from prison in 2011 for the 1978 murder. Russell Bufalino passed away on February 25, 1994 of a heart attack. He died in a nursing home a free man. My cousin Billy C.

passed away from a heart attack in 1997, this was one of the worse losses I have felt in my life, he was only 46 years old. We were as close as brothers most of our life.

In 1998, I was still working for American Airlines when a friend from Providence called me and made me aware of all the Tv and Film projects being done in RI and Boston. That I should come back up north get involved, this is where I earned my Screen Actors Guild card by performing in numerous project, such as, Waterfront, The Game Plan, Brotherhood, 27 Dresses, 21, Dan in Real Life, and several more in NYC.
I qualified for my SAG card but had to change my stage name from John Sullivan to Sean Collins because there had been 23 John Sullivan's working as actors over the years, and some were still collecting residuals from their film work after 40 years.

On Sept. 2, 2002 Cianci was sentenced to serve five years in Federal prison and was forced to resign again. He had plans to run for a 7th term as Mayor of Providence.

My Father's best friend for many years and his partner in many hits, Frank Sheeran passed away in December 2003, in a nursing home as a free man. This is where Frank made his peace with his maker, by telling author Charles Brant his life's story. Brant wrote the book "I Heard You Paint Houses". In that novel, there are numerous references to "Russell Bufalino" and my Dad "John Francis".

"Buckles" was released from Federal Prison and lives in North Providence. Anthony and Billy Blackjack are alive and well, living out their retirement in Rhode Island.

Always Be Daddy to Me

My relationship with my Father or just saying the name Daddy brings tears to my eyes. Something that I have done many times in 15 years since his death. I have never mourned my Father's death or my Mothers for that matter, I was there for them in death despite what may have occurred some 48 years earlier when they divorced. I was only five then, but always felt that I owed them respect for giving me the gift of life. I would return the favor in allowing them to die with respect and dignity by seeing that they had a proper funeral and burial. My mother passed first in Miami, my half-brother called and asked if we could have her service at my home in Dunedin Florida. This was the craziest weekend of my life. We had my Mom's service on a Friday, my oldest son John was getting married on Saturday the following day. We also had a baby shower planned for my daughter Kelly on Sunday afternoon. It was a crazy weekend of many different emotions. Most of the family would be in town for these events.

I never had a relationship with my mother since she dropped me on the sidewalk with my brown paper bag at the age of five to go live with my grandmother. Many years later I traveled to Houston, where she was living at the time and told her these three words, "I Forgive You". Nothing else needed to be said, she did not respond. She knew what I forgave her for.

We had a very nice service under a large tent along the Gulf of Mexico and then had her cremated. Although I only laid eyes on my mother 30 times over the years, it was like she saw my father's face when she looked at me and just the mentioning of my father's name would send her into a panic. She would look around to see if he was there. The word Daddy was so powerful and frightening to her even after 30 years. They were only married five years, but it was a nightmare to her. My father never put his hands on my mother she told me. But a short time into the marriage she slowly discovered who the man she was married to and the demons in his memories that would come out in his sleep and it scared her very much. My Dad was working for Meyer Lansky when I was born. She was later given the choice of uncontested divorce, she was never going to get custody of me or my sister. She ran as fast as she could, mom pulled away from the curb that morning at a high rate of speed, tires screeching. I can still see it and hear it like it was yesterday.

I did the same thing with my dad a few weeks later when I flew up to Providence to visit with him. He was sitting in his rocking chair watching his beloved Red Sox as he had done all his life, matter a fact and up until when he got ill with cancer the Red Sox and other sports related issues were the only subject we ever discussed. I went upstairs and said to him, "I Forgive You". He looked me in the eye and nodded his head in understanding and no verbal response.

My second wife who my father adored suggested that I go and tell my parents that I forgave them as a way of unloading my 1000 lbs. of shit and anger that I had carried around from that day when I was five. And by doing that it was for my own good, not theirs and it worked because I now felt free to live my life without all that resentment about my childhood. It was the greatest gift anyone had given me in my life. My wife Maryellen knew me better than I knew myself, Maryellen is my Soul Mate. In many way's she saved my life.

Became A New Man

My outlook on life became so different moving to Florida in 1989, the sun was out every day and believe me that makes you have a more positive outlook on life No ugly gray sky to wake up like the northeast, everything is beautiful all around you. Maryellen and I had to get away from Providence to start a new life together and my transfer to Tampa with American Airlines was the best thing that could happen to us. She had major family issues being the oldest girl of a family of 13 really put a lot of pressure on her to solve everyone's problems. I had a lot of the same issues with my family and we just had to get away and start fresh. We had five children between us from first marriages, only one Heather came with us in 1989. Slowly all five came to live with us in Florida, they were always flying on my free passes on vacations and holidays.

I had received my pension from the City of Providence in 1988,and then took a job with American Airlines in Boston as a part time fleet service clerk, baggage handler was my duties, but it was my way in the door to fulfill that dream I had as a child when my mother took off and left us with a Pilot from American Airlines back in the 1950s. I always wanted to travel and see the world, the world of those postcards my mother used to send me from places all over the world when they were traveling different places.

Well I stayed in Boston a short time and they allowed me to transfer to Providence Airport which was 40 miles closer to home. I worked in Providence for seven months, you had to spend six months in a city before you could put in for a transfer to another city that had an opening. My wife

Maryellen had lived in Florida in the past and loved it there, so we made several trips to see where we wanted to relocate to. We settled on the Tampa Bay area on the west coast near the water. We settled in Dunedin a small middleclass town just north of Clearwater. 20 miles from Tampa Airport where I would be working. Most of the guys I worked with were from the Northeast, so I felt right at home there. Florida was opposite of New England; the sun was out every day and it was cleaner and had much more beautiful scenery. Driving across causeways over Tampa Bay each day just put me in a different frame of mind. Working for an airline allows you to fly free when there are seats available, which we did numerous times back home to see my children and family,

I got involved in the Transport Workers Union that represents the employees against American Airlines. I say against because unions here in Florida where not very popular in this right to work state. I was elected to Sec Treasure of Local 554 which was the largest union in Florida at the time. Lots of travel and problems kept us busy fighting for small and large issues to protect our workers issues. As usual my mouth would get me in trouble all the time for speaking my mind and knowing how unions work in the northeast were they much stronger union states. They fought us tooth and nail just to honor the contract we were working under that they had signed.

A short time after in arrived in Tampa while working on the ramp after a summer thunder storm I was almost killed, by disconnecting a power unit from an aircraft while standing in water. The power unit discharged through my body and tore my shoulder nerves and elbow nerves and came out my left foot This was witnessed by a coworker who was driving push out tractor. It never healed right, and this was reason I was granted a disability pension years later.

We bought a Hair Salon on Main St in Dunedin and my wife worked 16 hours a day there to make ends meet. For first time in her life she was working for herself and she did a great job of it. Elegant Image was the name of the Salon. We rented out chairs to four operators, my job was to clean the shop every Sunday washing floors and other maintenance issues my wife could not handle. Maryellen was better at maintenance then me. We owned the business for seven years and then sold it. My wife got tired of the long hours and low pay.

Maryellen decided to fulfill her lifelong dream of becoming a Nurse. She started her long journey starting out her training as a CNA, then went on to LPN School. She worked as a LPN several years and then decided to become a RN and had to return to college to get her RN degree. When she puts her mind to something nothing can stop her I call her the Marathon Runner. She has worked as a Hospice RN for the last eight years or so. She feels she has found her calling in life helping her patients and their family in their most difficult time in their life. Between living with me for over 30yrs and the crap I have put her through and what she does for her patients daily has reserved a place in heaven next to God.

Four of our five children have followed us to Florida over the years and have their own family now and we have given us eight grandchildren. One son resides in California where he stayed after serving in the Marines for four years.

I retired in 2003 from the airline business and drove a school bus for almost five years just to stay busy. I mentored troubled teens for six years. Have gone out and spoke to teen groups about my life and have tried to be a positive example that I have made a good life for myself and family. Despite my early years and all the hurdles that I overcame with the help of many people from all sorts in life. I know at least 18 angels have come into my life some for very short periods and others for many years, but they always were positive influences on me. These people have all wanting me to do more with my life and not be like them, spending their life in jail or with a bullet in the back of their head. One example of angels walking among us is an older man that worked for Federal Towing in Providence back in 1983, I was very drunk one Friday night and drove a new auto into a pole, which I cut in half and I went through the windshield. I then proceeded to hit the gas thinking it was the brake, I went on to hit the hospital sign and transformer that knocked out power to hospital. I went through windshield a second time before hitting a wall. Glass was everywhere in my face eyes 70 stitches in my throat but otherwise ok. On the next day, I went to Federal Towing where my car was towed the night before to look at it. This little old man who had towed the car the night before came up to me and said I want you to come with me, we walked over to this big Lincoln which had no damage on it that I could see. The Man told me an 18-year-old boy had died last weekend in that car, when he hit the bridge of his nose on steering wheel.

He said follow me, so we can look at your car. I had no engine left in my big LTD, there was a big U all the way to the firewall from the pole I had hit. Old man says what do you think. "Time to stop drinking" and then he walks away I never seen the man again. I have never picked up a drink in 34 years since that Saturday morning... I got the message.

Many others have walked into my life and have tried to guide me in the right direction named Bufalino, Sheeran, Hoffa, Patriarca, Jerry T. JFK, Bianco, and Mr.

Lansky. I also had many great friends on the other side of the law, in law enforcement. Many that I grew up with on Smith Hill have been friends from childhood.

Making Our Peace with God

Some of this may be repetitive from my earlier writing but in the final eight months of Dad's life, he needed me to know that he may not have always been there, but he knew everything that happened blow by blow to all my craziness. My bond with Daddy was different as I grew older. I would call him Dad but somehow, he was always Daddy, the man that tried very hard to be my protector, not an easy chore considering all the trouble I would get myself into being so hyper and fearless. He seemed to be around the house at some of my worse moments. I recall several events when he was there for me, he got me out of fixes, carried me in his arms like a small child, stayed with me throughout the night and even went to bat for me on more than one occasion. Several of these events in the story I'm repeating as they were imbedded in my brain and by mentioning them again is only fitting as they show the love and compassion my dad and I had for one another. I know that the love a parent has for a child is beyond words, it's unconditional and when I think back on everything that happened between Dad and I it always brings a smile to my face and tears to my eyes all at the same time. I found that by reconnecting the dots of my life was his is a way of bringing closure to this great man. My Dad's long-term memory was sharp as a tack in the last eight months of his life while suffering with cancer again. He surprised me with memory of all the events that I put him through growing up. And he would lay there and go through them blow by blow or event by event.

When I was eight, he showed up on the river bank were my two friends had drowned. He also was there when I fell off the school wall onto an iron fence impaling myself in three locations. I pulled myself up off the fence somehow and two of the iron prongs went into my ass and the 3rd through my hand. My sister ran and got my father who was working on his auto in front of my grandmother house. He came running and screaming for me. He found me on the ground bleeding badly, he then picked me up in his arms and ran into traffic on Smith St which was the main road that ran in front of the Rhode Island State House. He ran in front of an auto that was being driven by a middle age woman, she stopped when my father told her my son is going to die if we don't get him to the hospital now, she opened the door and my dad placed me on the back seat, I was bleeding very badly my dad jumped in back with me. Then we sped to Roger Williams Hospital where my dad jumped out carrying me inside. I was taken to surgery and was operated on for several hours to stop the bleeding and to close the wounds. They told my father and I that if he had not got me to the hospital when he had, I would have bled out and died. I remember him looking at me and saying that I was going to be the death of him, then he grinned at me. I spent a week or so in the hospital and recovered fully but could not sit for quite a while. I later found out that my dad had given

$500 to the woman who drove us to the hospital because my blood had ruined her autos back seat.

My father was given custody of my sister and I and he made us go live with my grandmother, his mother Catherine Collins Sullivan on Jewett St where my mother had dropped us off that day and drove off. Rumors have it that my father was the first man ever given custody of the children over the woman in state history. My father's Lawyer was Joe Nugent who was elected Governor of Rhode Island a few years later. My father knew important people, or they knew him and respected him.

My earliest memories of when I would go in the Dew Drop Inn which was a lounge right across from the state house, we walk in and there were guys yelling out give bull what he was drinking and give "Cement" a soda, which was my first nickname from cracking my head on the sidewalk once and they men would tease me that I broke the cement. My father was a man of very few words, but he had many friends because guys always liked being around him.

My relationship was a strange one with him because he had an apartment across from the state house which I could see from my grandmother's house and very seldom allowed to go to his apartment. On one visit, there I started opening a big black foot locker he had there, he screamed at me to get away from there. That's my tools that I work with he yelled. You are going to give me a heart attack let's get out of here and he grabbed me by the hand and out we would go. Later many years later he told me the black locker where he kept his guns for his jobs. He was always traveling in and out of Providence all the time, sometimes for weeks at a time. He and my grandmother used to say he works for the railroad building bridges in Cn, and NYC.

I was very close to my grandmother and we spent a lot of time together and she loved me dearly and told me often, but she also said she did not know what to do with me and I was very often punished and told to go to bed till your father comes to talk to you and sometimes that was quite a few days. When he returned, he would talk to me, he never put his hands on me to punish me, I think he understood my issues with hyperactivity and incredible energy.

The first time I had a feeling my father was a bad ass was when someone tried to break into our house in the middle of the night and we lived on first floor and my grandmother and I slept in same bedroom. She woke me, and I grabbed the baseball bat and cracked whoever it was right in the head and they took off yelling. When my dad arrived a short time later, my grandmother yelled at him that "this must be about you, and you better take care of it". He returned later in different clothes on and Stated, "I took Care of it". It will never happen again believe me. He then pats me on the head said good job John, you take care of nana and your sister when I am not here.

On August 8, 1968 while standing on the street corner in front of the Pizza World an auto drove up to me and called me over and when I stuck my head in passenger window the driver fired two rounds right in my face somehow missing me and as I ran he fired four more shots at me, several friends were hit by the rounds that missed me. Later that night my father picked me up at police station with his lawyer and took me home to my grandmother's house. Everyone was up in arms because my cousin Ed Bannon had been there also and had been hit. Well everyone was screaming at my father as soon as we walked in. Then my Grandmother yells it must have been the IRA or some mobster that tried to kill your son. What the hell are you involved in now, she screamed at him you better fix this or I am going to kill you myself. If there was one person my father was afraid of it was Nana, she had grown up in Ireland when the war for Irish Independence was being fought. Led by her cousin Michael Collins and she knew what had to be done to put a stop to this crazy shit. This was the first time I was made aware of my family's history and my father's involvement in the mob.

All I ever heard about at that time was my father telling my grandmother that he had taken care of that little issue that needed to be resolved. He was a man of very few words but certainly a man of action.

Even though I was involved with my Dad's business over the years, I also attended those meetings at the office with Patriarca, Bufalino, and Frank. Shortly before the Hoffa thing and some other minor things our relationship never changed. We would talk mostly about sports and his Red sox until he got sick in 1983 with cancer for the first time.

I had told him that I forgave him several years earlier and it was now when he had cancer of the blood that he started talking to me about him being sorry and regretting many things from my childhood. He was sorry for driving my mother away because of who he was at the time, he told me he joined the Navy right out of high school at the age of 17 and he had talked Nana into signing the papers to join. He was sent to the Pacific and to a PT boat which went from one island to next chasing the JAPS as he called them among many other worse things. He said they were not human beings they were the devil's children for what they did to the US soldiers on the Baton March. They would string up and hang soldiers and citizens for all to see. And that experience changed him to the point of becoming numb to killing another person back in the states. He said nine out of ten deserved to get wacked anyways because they were scum bags anyways.

For the first time I was talking to Daddy and he was giving me a better understanding of why our childhood was the way it was; a lot of heavy duty shit went on, but no one ever talked about it. Everything was a secret and kept close to the vest as they would say. And now I was getting a blow by blow explanation of my life and certain events that played out like a video rerun because my father was really trying to make amends for every difficulty I went through. Like the 68 shooting that fucked my head so bad that I started drinking, quit high school, started stealing and giving people beatings and such, which in turn forced me to join military to try to get back on track and having my own bad experience in the Army in Vietnam. When I returned, I found myself involved with the Mob myself and my father's friends.

Despite the subject matters my dad would tell me and I counted at least 14 hits that he was involved in with Frank and others for Patriarca and his mentor Russell Bufalino. I felt closeness to my father that had never existed before. I really felt gratified that my father was sharing his deepest darkest secrets with me, which made me feel like I was the most important person in his life for the first time because he needed to talk to someone and because he was trying to make his peace with his maker.

As he was getting sicker with the cancer and it had reached his head, my visits were many and the stories and details would flow like water. His friendship with Frank Sheeran and Russell was always front and center because of the trust they had after being hounded by the Hoffa disappearance for several years about their involvement and the aftermath to keep it secret. My dad never made excuses about what he did in his life and he said he always made peace with the event a short time afterwards with himself and God. I never judged my father for anything he told me had occurred and I felt that he was giving me a gift of getting to know him like no other person ever had. He would say from time to time, "I Did What I Had to Do". All the events that are discussed in this book are mine and my father's truth, He was using me to make his peace with himself and his God and he also always felt that America was entitled to know the truth about events from the 60s and 70s because he felt used by many people who had no morals and had never fought in wartime, and they changed

American history over greed. He always regretting giving Nixon all those bags of cash from Hoffa in DC.

I have two regrets regarding my father's passing away. The cancer had reached my father's brain and they said he had 30 days at the most to live. I made a dozen trips from Tampa to Providence to spend time with my father and let him make his peace with God by telling me everything and I brought a Catholic priest in to take my father's confession two weeks before he passed away.

On one of my last visits we were alone in the nursing home on his bed when he asked me to talk to his present wife Betty about allowing him to go home to die in his own bed or chair just, so he could be comfortable. Well my wife and I offered to stay with him till he passed. My wife being a nurse was going to take a leave of absent to care for him. I witnessed my Daddy cry for the first time in my life begging me to get her to change her mind. She said no. I said I would move him she said she would call the cops on me. I left the nursing home and my dad had passed out on his bed so when I left I felt I had let him down, it was also the first time my dad had ever asked me for something in my life and I could not deliver.

The second regret was the last time I'd seen him alive, as he died on a Sunday morning while I was flying from Tampa to be with him because I just had this feeling that he wanted to tell me something else to help him make his peace with God. My sister and cousins met me at the RI airport and as I came down the ramp my heart just dropped, and I knew the man I called Daddy was gone.

We waked my dad and buried him in East Providence at Gates of Heaven Cemetery. I left the same day to go back home with my wife in our auto because she had driving up with the children.

My dad had been as many New Englanders had been waiting for the Red Sox to win the World Series since 1912 or so. Every year they would always say oh just wait until next year everyone would say. Now if you are not from New England you do not understand because how the Sox do each night will affect the next day. It will make you angry, depressed or you will be on cloud nine because they won and have great day. Well my dad had been waiting for over 50 years to see his beloved Sox win, he didn't get that opportunity before he died the previous year.

In 2004 when the Red Sox finally won the Series, I was living in Dunedin, Florida but my heart and memories were back in Boston with all my people when the Sox got the final out. I broke down like a weeping child that I used to be when the Sox would break our hearts year after year. I was not weeping for joy of the great win of the Sox but weeping because my father did not live long enough to see his beloved Sox win it all. It was tough few days despite being happy as a pig in shit over the win but also having a heavy heart.

Several weeks later I flew up to Providence to visit my dad's grave in East Providence, which was in same cemetery Raymond Patriarca was buried. Raymond was in a large tomb you could see it from half mile away. Dad was in a flat in the ground plot that I always had to uncover when there was snow on the ground. I had stopped and bought a Red Sox flag to put next to headstone and to my amazement there were hundreds of flags and other mementos everywhere. I found his site and dropped to my knees and put his flag in the ground and totally went to pieces. I laid by his grave and cried away while talking to him about the Sox winning because most of my life that was the one bond we always had was our love of the Red Sox. We would talk endless day and night about them, but this came to a screeching halt later in life. When Dad finally became very ill and allowed me inside his head and heart. I would sit with him and just be there to listen and not judge him, to accept his heartfelt apology for the life I had to live because of his actions he took in his life.

Even with all the horrid stories, I felt that it was a gift to me from him, it gave me a better understanding of events that he and no one else ever talked about. The Family's answer was always "Your Father took care of it".

All in all, I am writing this story about the many people that help guide me, chewed my ass off, watched over me, gave me jobs and even give me advice to not be like them. They often said you're better than us kid and to do something with my life and something to make them proud. "So, this my Story and I'm Sticking To it". It will never be a typical mobster story because none has ever taken the time to see the good in everyone and I was given the gift for seeing into many good souls and I believe it is God's Plan for me to complete this project.

After 19 near death experiences I have lived through in my life, I truly believe that by me telling this fantastic story of the events of the 20th Century, is the work that God has wanted me to finish before my time on this earth is up.

Made in the USA
Middletown, DE
16 August 2018